I'd like to thank my parents and my husband for buying
into my dream for children's books. Ever since I can
remember I have wanted to write and illustrate for children
and to be able to live this every day is a dream come true.

- SM

First American Edition 2020
Kane Miller, A Division of EDC Publishing
www.kanemiller.com
First published in Great Britain 2020 by Caterpillar Books Ltd,
an imprint of the Little Tiger Group
Text by Patricia Hegarty
Text copyright © Caterpillar Books Ltd 2020
Illustrations copyright © Sakshi Mangal 2020
Library of Congress Control Number: 2019941832
Printed in China
ISBN: 978-1-68464-055-3
CPB/1400/1300/0919
10 9 8 7 6 5 4 3 2 1

Best BEHAVIOR

Written by
Patricia Hegarty

Illustrated by
Sakshi Mangal

Kane Miller
A DIVISION OF EDC PUBLISHING

When you get up in the **morning**,

At the start of
a brand-new **day**,

Get **washed** and **brush** your teeth carefully,

And your bright smile will **light** up your **way.**

Getting dressed can sometimes be **tricky**—

All those
buttons
can be
such a **pain.**

Don't get in a **tangle** with **laces,**

And **remember** to comb your **wild mane!**

And now it's time
to eat **breakfast,**

The most important meal of the **day.**

You need **food** to fill you with **energy**,

So you'll be able to run around and **play**.

As you're going
to school now,

It's important to
look and **take care.**

If you cross roads with lots of **traffic,**

You need eyes and ears **everywhere!**

"Good morning, everyone!"

There's a proper place for **everything,**

It's something we all find out.

Hang up
your coat
and your
scarf,
please,

Don't leave things
lying **about!**

In the playground
it's very **important,**

Not to push others
out of the **way.**

If you can learn to **play nicely,**

Then everyone has a **good day.**

Even the **hungriest** hippo
Has a difficult lesson to **learn**.

It's no use being
impatient,

Stand in line
and wait for
your **turn**.

At home, when you've finished **playing**,

And **toys** are all **over** the **house**,

Take time
to help with
the **tidying**—

Behave like a
good little **mouse!**

After play, it's nearly
dinnertime,

But remember before we **begin,**

We must
always
wash
our hands
first,

Once we've done that, we can **tuck in!**

Now that it's finally **bath time,**

You can splash
around and have **fun.**

Don't forget to **wash** behind your ears,

And wrap up **warm**

when you're **done.**

Now you're clean and ready for **bedtime,**

Settle in and
snuggle up
tight.

There'll be a
good night kiss
and a **story,**

Before it's time
to turn out
the **light**.

That's another busy day over,

The moon and stars are **shining bright.**

There's nothing left for you to do,

Close your eyes,

sweet dreams, **good night.**